For Hershey—
my sister's precious pup

Henry Holt and Company, LLC
Publishers since 1866
175 Fifth Avenue
New York, New York 10010
www.HenryHoltKids.com

Henry Holt® is a registered trademark
of Henry Holt and Company, LLC.
Copyright © 2008 by Denise Fleming
All rights reserved.
Distributed in Canada by H. B. Fenn and Company Ltd.

Library of Congress Cataloging-in-Publication Data
Fleming, Denise.
Buster goes to Cowboy Camp / Denise Fleming.—1st ed.
p.   cm.
Summary: When Buster the dog's owner goes away for a few days,
he sends Buster to Sagebrush Kennels for Cowboy Camp, where
Buster is homesick at first, but then has fun herding balls into the corral,
gathering sticks for a campfire, and making wanted posters with his pawprints.
ISBN-13: 978-0-8050-7892-3 / ISBN-10: 0-8050-7892-4
[1. Dogs—Fiction. 2. Camps—Fiction. 3. Homesickness—Fiction.] I. Title.
PZ7.F5994Bus 2008   [E]—dc22   2007012368

First Edition—2008
Printed in the United States of America on acid–free paper. ∞

10   9   8   7   6   5   4   3   2   1

The illustrations were created by pouring colored cotton fiber through hand-cut stencils.
Book design by Denise Fleming and David Powers.

Visit www.denisefleming.com.

Henry Holt and Company
New York

BUSTER
goes to Cowboy Camp

Denise Fleming

Not Happy

Buster was not happy.

Brown Shoes was going away for a weekend of rest and relaxation.

Betty was staying with Mrs. Pink Slippers next door.

Mrs. Pink Slippers loved cats.

Mrs. Pink Slippers did not feel the same way about dogs.

Buster

So, Buster was going to Cowboy Camp
at Sagebrush Kennels.
Buster did not want to go to Cowboy Camp.
Buster was worried about sleeping away from home.

Good-bye

Brown Shoes handed Buster's dishes to Red Boots.
Brown Shoes patted Buster on the head,
told Buster he'd see him in a few days,
and drove away.

Buster's stomach flip-flopped.
Buster missed Brown Shoes and Betty already.

Yee Haw!

Red Boots welcomed Buster to Sagebrush Kennels with a big cowboy howdy.
Red Boots tied a blue bandanna around Buster's neck
and gave Buster the tenderfoot tour of the camp.

mesquite trees

fence

Red Boots showed Buster the chuck wagon where Buster would get his chow, the corral for herding and roping, and the bunkhouse where Buster would sleep.

Red Boots told Buster to get some shut-eye as the next day was fixin' to be a busy one.

office

cacti

windmill

toolshed

Sagebrush Kennels

swimming hole

chuck wagon

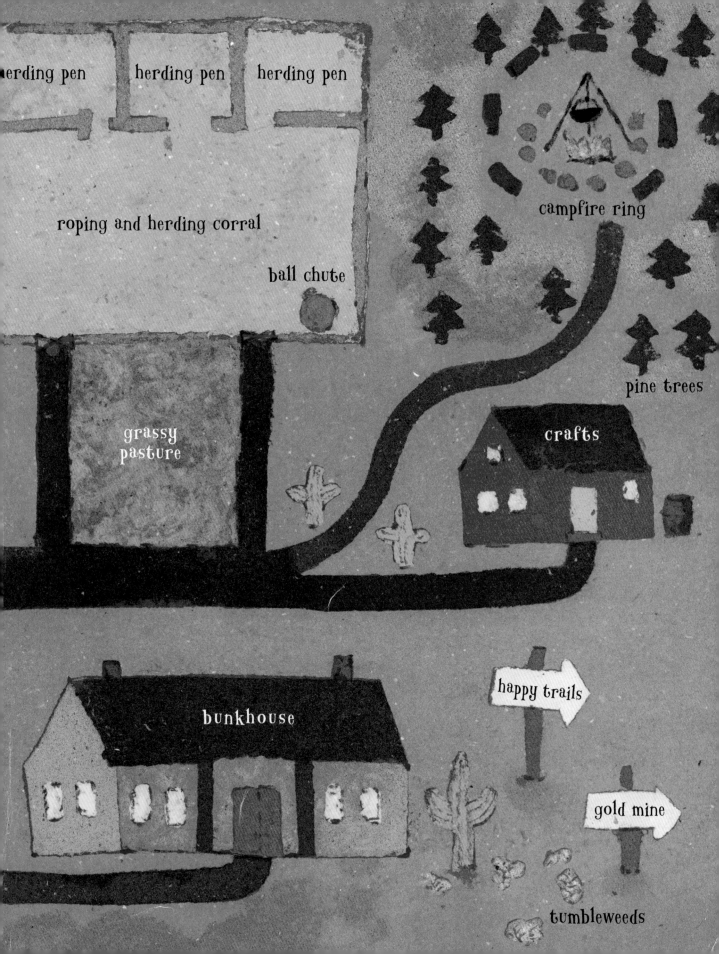

Homesick

Buster looked around the bunkhouse.
The dog in the next bed was sleeping.
Sleeping and snoring and *drooling*.
Buster moved to the edge of his bunk.

Buster had a hard time getting to sleep.
The bed was lumpy.
There were strange smells and sounds.

Buster missed Betty's purring.
He missed the bedtime snack
he always shared with Brown Shoes.
Buster was not happy.

Buster was homesick.

Morning

Buster heard the rattle of dishes.

He opened his eyes.

It was already morning.

He looked at the dog in the next bed.

The dog looked back and smiled.

Buster felt a bit better.

Buster ate a few bites of breakfast.
Then he went in search of Red Boots.

Red Boots had set out pots of brightly colored paint and large sheets of white paper with the word **WANTED** printed across the bottom. Buster dipped the tip of his paw in the paint and dabbed the paper.

Buster dipped another paw in the paint and dabbed the paper.

Buster dipped all four paws in the paint and danced across the paper.

Red Boots hung Buster's wanted poster on the fence.

Roundup

Red Boots opened a chute, and balls of different sizes came bouncing out.

The campers started running and jumping, herding the balls into pens in the corral.

A big red ball came bouncing toward Buster.

Buster ducked behind a fence post.

Buster was not good at games.

Buckaroo Ball

Red Boots called Buster over to play buckaroo ball.
Buster pretended to study a butterfly.

Red Boots called Buster's name again.
Buster acted as if he did not hear Red Boots.

Out of the corner of his eye Buster saw a ball coming his way.
Buster turned his head,
opened his mouth to yelp,

and . . .

thunk!

Buster caught the ball!

thunk!

thunk!

Buster caught the ball again and again.
Maybe Buster wasn't so bad at games after all.

Sunset

Buster gathered sticks.
He helped Red Boots build a campfire.

Red Boots hung a big kettle of beans and bacon over the fire.

Red Boots sat by the fire, played the guitar,
and sang cowboy songs as supper cooked.
Buster sang along.

Red Boots ladled beans and bacon into Buster's bowl.
Buster's favorite part of supper was the bacon.
Before Buster knew it the day was over.

Hit the Hay

Red Boots told the cowpokes it was time to hit the hay—
tomorrow was fixin' to be another busy day.
They were going to be digging for gold,
practicing rope tricks, and making shiny sheriff's badges.

Buster could hardly wait!

Pardners

Buster walked back to the bunkhouse with Snarkle,
the dog from the next bunk.
Before the lights were out, Buster was sleeping.
Sleeping, snoring, and . . .
drooling.